Animal Hours

by
Linda Manning

illustrated by
Vlasta van Kampen

TORONTO   OXFORD   NEW YORK
OXFORD UNIVERSITY PRESS

Oxford University Press, 70 Wynford Drive, Don Mills, Ontario, M3C 1J9

Toronto Oxford New York Delhi Bombay Calcutta Madras Karachi
Petaling Jaya Singapore Hong Kong Tokyo Nairobi Dar es Salaam
Cape Town Melbourne Auckland

and associated companies in
Berlin Ibadan

Canadian Cataloguing in Publication Data

Manning, Linda
Animal hours

ISBN 0-19540771-7 (bound) ISBN 0-19-540844-6 (pbk.)

1. Time – Juvenile literature. 2. Time measurements –
Juvenile literature. I. Van Kampen, Vlasta.
II. Title.

QB209.5.M36 1990   j529'.7   C90-093344-5

Text © Linda Manning 1990
Illustrations © Vlasta van Kampen 1990

Oxford is a trademark of Oxford University Press
1 2 3 4 – 3 2 1 0

Printed in Singapore

For my mother,

— Linda

For Jan,
my mentor, friend and husband.

— Vlasta

What if . . .
An elephant asked to play hopscotch at one!

Would her feet be too big?
Would it be any fun?

A chimpanzee wanted a haircut at two!

Would you trim it or shave it?
What would you do?

A tall giraffe grabbed your two-wheeler at three!

Would she bump into something?
And skin her left knee?

What if . . .
A huge lion joined you for TV at four?

Would monster shows scare him?
Would he hug you and roar?

A fat hippo splashed in your pool around five!

Would you jump in and join her?
Would you think she should dive?

A slippery seal came for supper at six!

Would he have any manners?
Or try to do tricks?

What if . . .
A polar bear squeezed in your bathtub at seven!

Would it take long to scrub her?
Perhaps till eleven?

A kangaroo bounced through your bedroom at eight!

Should you read her a story?
Or yawn, ''It's too late.''

A slinky snake slid from your closet at nine!

Should you hide in the covers?
Or would you be fine?

What if . . .
An oppossum hung from your bedpost at ten!

Would his snoring disturb you,
Again and again?

A sleepy owl swooped overhead at eleven!

And hooted this lullaby,
"Sleep well till seven!"

BUT THEN what if . . .
A tiny mouse set your alarm off at twelve!

And started to tap dance
On top of the shelves,

And handed out party hats streamers and all

Blew up balloons and cried,
"Let's have a ball!"

And boogied and bunny-hopped till the first light,

Then curtseyed quite sweetly
And whispered . . .

"Good night!"